HERE COMES
THE BUS!

J
H

By the Same Author

Published by William Morrow and Company

SNOWBOUND WITH BETSY. 1962
ANNIE PAT AND EDDIE. 1960
EDDIE AND LOUELLA. 1959
BETSY'S WINTERHOUSE. 1958
EDDIE MAKES MUSIC. 1957
BETSY'S BUSY SUMMER. 1956
EDDIE AND HIS BIG DEALS. 1955
BETSY AND THE CIRCUS. 1954
EDDIE'S PAY DIRT. 1953
THE MIXED-UP TWINS. 1952
EDDIE AND GARDENIA. 1951
BETSY'S LITTLE STAR. 1950
EDDIE AND THE FIRE ENGINE. 1949
PENNY GOES TO CAMP. 1948
LITTLE EDDIE. 1947

Published by Harcourt, Brace and World

PENNY AND PETER. 1946
BETSY AND THE BOYS. 1945
HERE'S A PENNY. 1944
BACK TO SCHOOL WITH BETSY. 1943
PRIMROSE DAY. 1942
BETSY AND BILLY. 1941
TWO AND TWO ARE FOUR. 1940
"B" IS FOR BETSY. 1939

HERE COMES THE BUS!

written and illustrated by
CAROLYN HAYWOOD

William Morrow and Company
New York   1963

J
H

To:

> Disty,
> Stanley,
> Neddie,
> and
> Hoddy,

my young neighbors and
ever-ready helpers.

Any resemblance between **Mr. Riley** the bus driver and **Bud Wood** of **Rockland, Maine,** is purely intentional and is the result of the author's personal acquaintance with **Bud** and his **Owls Head** school bus.

CONTENTS

1.   Here Comes the Bus!   15

2.   First Day of School   34

3.   Taffy and His Shoes   51

4.   The Forgotten Birthday Cake   68

5.   Who's Got the Cake?   84

6.   The Pumpkin People   100

7.   The Christmas Tree   121

8.   Walking on the Snow Piles   138

9.   The Pet Show   156

10.   A Surprise for Jonathan   171

HERE COMES
THE BUS!

Chapter One

HERE COMES THE BUS!

IT WAS an early morning in October. It was very early. The sun had just come up. The air was chilly, almost cold. Jonathan Mason stood by the side of the road. He was wearing his new school trousers and a blue jacket. His new schoolbag hung over his shoulder. Cocoa, his cocker spaniel, stood beside him. He was called Cocoa because he was white with soft brown spots, the color of cocoa.

Cocoa had come to live with Jonathan when they were both five months old, so Jonathan could not remember a time when Cocoa had not lived with him. Now they were both five years old, almost six.

Jonathan was waiting for the school bus. Cocoa didn't know what he was waiting for. He was just waiting, because Jonathan was waiting. He didn't need any other reason.

Jonathan looked up the road. He would know the school bus right away, because it was bright yellow. He had seen the bus the day before, when his mother had driven him to his new school to look at it. He hadn't stayed, because school was almost over for the day, but his name was put down in the first grade.

As Jonathan had wriggled into the seat beside his

16

mother, in her car, he said, "Look, Mommy! Look at the bus. Is that the bus that will take me to school?"

"Yes, Jon!" said his mother. "Every morning the bus will stop for you at the corner of our lane. It will bring you back every afternoon."

"I mustn't miss the bus," said Jonathan.

"You won't miss it," said his mother. "I'll take you to the end of our lane. I'll wait with you until the bus comes."

"Oh, no, Mommy!" Jonathan had exclaimed. "You mustn't! I want to go by myself."

"Oh! Very well!" his mother had replied, looking at him out of the corner of her eye. Jonathan looked very little, but she guessed that he felt big now that he was in the first grade.

Standing alone, with Cocoa, at the end of the lane, waiting for the school bus, Jonathan didn't feel very big. After all, he *wasn't* very big. He wasn't much taller

17

than the two mailboxes by the road. It was very quiet and he felt lonely. No cars passed on the road. No trucks went by.

Jonathan looked back toward his house. He could not see it. It was hidden by trees. Golden leaves fell from the trees. They didn't make any sound. He guessed that his father and mother were still asleep. He had washed and dressed himself very quietly, and he had closed the front door carefully when he left the house, so as not to waken them.

Jonathan began to feel hungry. He hadn't had any breakfast. He put his hand into the pocket of his trousers. His fingers touched something small and round. He pulled out a red gumdrop. Jonathan ate the gumdrop. It was the first time he had ever eaten a gumdrop for breakfast.

He looked up the road to see if the bus was coming. The road was empty. Away off to one side, he could see a farmhouse. A great tall tree stood beside the farm-

house. Its leaves had turned bright red. The morning sun, shining on the tree, made it fire bright. As far as Jonathan could see on both sides of the road, there were fields. "Farmland," Daddy called it.

Jonathan had just come to live in the country. He had always lived on the edge of a big city. His father wrote books and wanted to be where it was very quiet, so he had found a nice farmhouse in the country. A farmer who lived nearby was going to farm the land that Jonathan's father had bought with the house. The Masons had expected to move into the house long before school opened in September, but the painters had been very slow putting the last coat of paint on the walls. So it was the first of October before Jonathan and his father and mother and Cocoa were settled in their new home.

Now, at last, Jonathan was going to his new school. He stood first on one foot, then on the other, waiting for the bus. As he waited, he began to get a very queer feeling. It was a feeling he had never had before. His tummy seemed to be jumping up and down.

Jonathan felt all mixed up. He didn't know what he wanted. One minute he looked up the road for the school bus, wanting it to come. The next minute he was afraid to look, for fear he would see the big bus coming over the hill.

After all, he had never been on a school bus before. He had only been on big city buses, and his mother had been with him every time. He remembered that once he had been on a big city bus with his mother, and the bus driver had been mean to Mommy. He had yelled at her, because she couldn't find her money. She had dropped it into the bottom of a big shopping bag. The bus driver had put them off the bus, and it had been raining very hard with thunder and lightning. Jonathan had cried, because he was frightened.

Everyone in the bus had looked down from the windows at them as the bus drove on. The people inside the bus were nice and dry, but he and Mommy, standing outside, were wet as dishmops. Since then Jonathan had not cared for bus drivers. He wondered why bus drivers couldn't be as nice as his friend the milkman.

One of Jonathan's best friends had been Mr. Riley, the milkman who had delivered milk to the house where Jonathan had lived before. The only reason he was sorry to move away from the city was that he would not see Mr. Riley anymore.

Mr. Riley had often taken Jonathan riding in the milk truck. It was fun to go with him. They met a great many dogs as they went around delivering milk. Jonathan liked dogs, and Mr. Riley knew all of their names. Mr. Riley called Jonathan, Jonny. He was the only person who ever called him that. Sometimes he called him Jonny Cake. Everyone else called him Jon.

Jonathan's thoughts went back to bus drivers. Suddenly he remembered that he did not have any money.

He felt in all his pockets. He did not find a single penny.

Jonathan turned and ran down the lane as fast as he could go, back to the house. He hadn't any money to pay the bus driver! The bus driver would be mean to him! He would put him off the bus, and he would be late for school! Jonathan's legs flew and Cocoa flew beside him, his long ears streaming out on each side of his head.

When they reached the house, the front door was locked. Jonathan pounded on the door. He was out of breath and all he could think was, I'll miss the bus! I'll miss the bus! I'll be late for school! He pounded on the door harder. *Bang, bang, bang!* Cocoa barked louder, "Bow, wow, wow!"

Suddenly the door was pulled open, and there stood Jonathan's father, in his pajamas. He had shaving cream all over his face. Behind him was Jonathan's mother, in her bathrobe. She had her toothbrush in her hand.

"Jon!" said his father. "What are you doing out here so early in the morning?"

Jonathan rushed into the house. "I haven't any money for the bus fare!" he cried. "The bus driver will put me off the bus! I'll be late for school!"

"Jon!" said his mother. "It will be a whole hour before the bus comes. You haven't had your breakfast, and I have to pack your lunch."

"Oh!" said Jonathan, sounding like air coming out of a balloon. He sat down on the bottom step of the stairs and waited for his father and mother to dress.

His mother came down first. "Jon, honey!" she said. "You don't have to have money for bus fare."

"You mean, it's free?" said Jonathan.

"Yes, it's free," his mother replied.

"Oh!" said Jonathan.

"Now come and eat your breakfast," said his mother.

"I had a gumdrop," said Jonathan.

"A gumdrop isn't very much for breakfast," said his mother, as she started to boil an egg on the stove.

While Jonathan ate his breakfast, his mother packed his lunch box. It was made of tin and looked like a tiny suitcase. Into the box she put a peanut-butter sandwich, two sugar cookies, and an apple.

"I never took my lunch before, did I?" said Jonathan.

"No," replied his mother. "You came home every day for lunch when you went to kindergarten."

"It's like going on a picnic, isn't it?" said Jonathan.

"A little," his mother answered, "but on a picnic you can't buy a bowl of soup."

Jonathan laughed. "Am I going to buy a bowl of soup?" he asked.

"Yes!" said his mother. "I'm putting ten cents into the box. That is for the bowl of soup."

"Where do I buy it?" Jonathan asked.

"Your teacher will tell you," said his mother.

"I never bought a bowl of soup before," said Jonathan. "I hope I don't spill it."

"Oh, no!" said his mother. "Not on your first day at school!"

"I'll hold my breath," said Jonathan, as he got up from the breakfast table.

"Everything will be all right," said his mother.

"Well, I guess I better go," said Jonathan.

"The bus won't come for twenty-five minutes," said his mother.

"Is that long?" Jonathan asked.

"It's too long to stand by the road and wait."

"All right," said Jonathan, "I'll give Cocoa a Yummie for his breakfast."

It didn't take Cocoa more than a minute to eat his Yummie. When he had finished, Jonathan played with him for a few more minutes. Then he picked up his lunch box, and said, "Well, I guess I better go."

"Not yet, Jon!" said his mother.

"I want to see the bus come over the hill," said Jonathan. "It might come early."

"Very well!" said his mother. "Cocoa, you stay here." Cocoa lowered his head and went under the kitchen table. He looked very sad.

Jonathan had his hand on the doorknob of the front door. Then he turned back. In a moment he was standing in the doorway of the kitchen. "Mommy!" he said.

"What is it, Jon?" his mother asked.

"Do you think the bus driver will be nice?" he asked.

"Oh, I'm sure he will be nice," his mother replied.

"Not as nice as Mr. Riley, though," said Jonathan.

"Perhaps so," said his mother. "Perhaps he will be even nicer than Mr. Riley."

Jonathan shook his head. "Bus drivers are never as nice as milkmen," he said.

"Oh, come, come! Just wait!" said his mother. "I'm sure this bus driver is a nice bus driver."

Jonathan made no reply as he went out to wait for the bus at the end of the lane. He stood a long time, looking up the road at the top of the hill.

Suddenly he saw the bus. It was coming over the hill. It was a much brighter yellow than he remembered when he had seen it standing outside the school the day before. The sun shining on it turned its windshield to bright gold.

Jonathan's tummy began jumping around again. For a moment, he wanted to turn and run back down the lane, but he knew he could not do that. He had to go to school. Then he wished that his mother had come with him, but it was too late to get her. The bus seemed to be flying toward him. Now it was here. It stopped smoothly. The door opened right in front of Jonathan.

"Hi!" said the bus driver. "Come on in."

Jonathan stepped into the bus and looked into the face of the bus driver.

"Hi! You're Jonny!" said the bus driver. "I'm glad

31

to see you. You sit over there beside that old-timer."
The bus driver pointed to a boy not much bigger than
Jonathan. "He's in the second grade."

Jonathan didn't say a word. He sat down, but he
did not take his eyes off the bus driver. The bus driver
looked just like Mr. Riley.

At last Jonathan found his tongue. He said to the
boy next to him, "What's his name?"

"Whose?" said the boy.

"The bus driver's," said Jonathan.

"Mr. Wiley," replied the boy, "but I call him, Wus.
What's your name?"

"Jonathan," he answered, "but everybody calls me
Jon, except Mr. Riley. He called me Jonny."

"Sure 'nough!" said the boy. "I heard him."

Jonathan looked puzzled, but he said, "What's your
name?"

"Woland," said the boy. "Woland Walston."

"Do you like bus drivers?" Jonathan whispered.

32

"Sure!" was the reply. "I like Wus."

When the bus reached the school, the children jumped out. Jonathan's new friend called back, "Good-by, Wus!"

Jonathan said, "Good-by, Mr. Wiley."

"So long, Jonny!" the bus driver called after him. "See you this afternoon."

Chapter Two

FIRST DAY OF SCHOOL

As soon as Jonathan stepped out of the bus he was alone. All the children rushed off to join someone they knew. "Hi!" they shouted. "Hi, Davy! Hi, Pete! Hi, Fatso!" they called to each other. No one called out, "Hi, Jon!" Even Jonathan's new friend he had met on the bus ran away like everyone else.

34

Jonathan stood holding his lunch box. He looked around at the laughing, shouting children. He only saw strange faces. There was no boy he could call by name. No girl, either. Everybody knew everybody, but nobody knew Jonathan.

Then Jonathan saw the bus driver coming toward him. A little girl ran beside the bus driver, keeping up with his long steps. When they reached him, Jonathan called out, "Hi, Mr. Wiley!" He was very glad he had someone to call to.

"Hi, Jonny!" said the bus driver. "Here's a girl who is in your class. This is Melissa." Then he looked down at Melissa, and said, "Melissa, this is Jonathan."

"Hello, Jonathan," said Melissa. "I saw you when your mother brought you to school yesterday."

"Hi!" replied Jonathan. "Everyone calls me Jon."

"Well, come on, Jon," said Melissa. "You can go into school with me." Melissa took tight hold of Jonathan's hand. "Come on," she said.

Jonathan didn't budge. "Let go! Let go!" he said. "I want to go by myself." Jonathan pulled his hand away from Melissa's.

"Well, I'll carry your lunch box for you," said Melissa, grabbing hold of Jonathan's lunch box.

"I can carry it," said Jonathan. "I want to carry it."

Just then the bell rang for the children to go into school. "Come on!" said Melissa. "Hurry up! That's the bell."

"I know!" said Jonathan. "Give me my lunch box." Jonathan had never owned a lunch box before, and he was proud of it.

Melissa wasn't listening. She went off with Jonathan's lunch box in one hand and her bag in the other. Jonathan ran along beside her calling, "Give me my lunch box!"

Melissa began to run toward the door of the school. When she reached the steps, she tripped and fell. Jonathan's lunch box popped open. His apple flew one way.

36

His sandwich flew another way. His cookies and his dime fell out. A boy ran up behind Jonathan and Melissa. He didn't mean to kick the apple, but he did. It hit the wall and broke into pieces.

Melissa picked herself up. "Oh, dear! Oh, dear!" she said. Then she took a step backward and stepped right on Jonathan's sandwich. "Oh, dear!" cried Melissa, looking down at her feet. "Now look! I have peanut butter on my new shoe."

"Well, look at my sandwich!" said Jonathan. "What about my sandwich?"

"Here are your cookies," said another little girl, handing Jonathan his package of cookies. They were still wrapped in the wax paper, but they had broken into little bits.

"Is this your dime?" a boy asked, picking it up.

Jonathan picked up his lunch box and looked inside it. "I guess it is," he said. "I don't see it in my lunch box."

Just then Jonathan's teacher, Miss Adams, opened the door. When she saw the crowd of children around Jonathan, she said, "Now what's going on here? Where is the first-grade line?"

"Melissa fell down," said the boy who had picked up the dime.

"She took my lunch box," said Jonathan. "And she stepped on my sandwich."

"I was helping him," said Melissa. "I was just helping him."

"Perhaps Jonathan didn't want to be helped, Melissa," said Miss Adams.

"I didn't," said Jonathan.

"Come now," said Miss Adams, putting Jonathan at the head of the line. The first grade straightened up. "Follow me, Jonathan," said Miss Adams.

Jonathan followed Miss Adams, and the rest of the children followed Jonathan. They walked through the

hall to the first-grade classroom. Jonathan carried his lunch box with the broken cookies in one hand and his dime in the other. I can still have a bowl of soup, he thought.

At lunchtime Miss Adams led the children to the lunchroom. It was filled with long tables and long benches. At one end of the room there was a counter. Two women in white dresses and white aprons stood behind the counter. Jonathan smelled a nice odor of food. He guessed it was the soup.

Melissa rushed up to Jonathan, and said, "Here, Jon, you can have one of my sandwiches, 'cause I stepped on yours."

"Thanks!" said Jonathan. "What kind is it?"

"It's nut bread with apple butter," Melissa replied.

"Thanks!" said Jonathan again. "I have ten cents for a bowl of soup, too."

"I'll get it for you," said Melissa.

Jonathan let out a cry. "No! No! I'll get it, Molasses! I'll get it, Molasses!"

Melissa opened her eyes very wide. Then she opened her mouth and cried, "My name is not *Molasses!* My name is Melissa!"

Every child in the lunchroom heard her. They all began to laugh, and the boys cried out, "Melissa Molasses! Melissa Molasses!" The children laughed harder, and even Melissa laughed.

Jonathan got his own bowl of soup, and he did not drop it. He ate Melissa's sandwich with the soup. Jonathan thought he had never eaten such good soup and such a good sandwich. When he finished, he said to Melissa, "That was a good sandwich. I'm glad you stepped on my peanut-butter sandwich."

At three o'clock, when it was time to go home, Miss Adams led the children out to the school bus. The bus

driver was standing beside the door. When the children saw him, they called out, "Hi! Hello! Who rides on the hot seat?" The big heater in the bus made a nice seat right beside Mr. Riley. Every child loved to ride on the hot seat.

"Who rides on the hot seat, Miss Adams?" the bus driver asked.

"Put Jon on the hot seat," Melissa called out.

"Yes, Jon rides on the hot seat!" several children called at once.

"I don't want to ride on a hot seat," said Jon.

"Sure you do!" Melissa said. "Everybody wants to ride on the hot seat."

"Hop in!" said the bus driver.

Jonathan stepped into the bus. Melissa and the rest of the children pushed in behind him. "This is it!" said Melissa. "This is the hot seat." She pointed to a box that was right beside the driver's seat. "Sit down! Sit down!" said Melissa.

45

Jonathan looked at the seat. He wondered how hot it would be. He looked worried. His forehead was full of wrinkles. He didn't like the idea of sitting on a hot stove.

"It's all right, Jonny," said the bus driver. "Sit down."

"Is it very hot?" Jonathan asked.

"Not now," replied the driver. "It's hot in the wintertime when it's cold outside. Then everybody wants to ride on it."

"Oh!" said Jonathan with a sigh. He sat down. The seat didn't feel hot at all. It was a good seat, because he could watch the road just as the driver did.

All the way it was stop and go, stop and go. At each stop one child, and sometimes more than one, jumped out of the bus. Jonathan hoped that Mr. Wiley would know when to put him off, because every lane looked the same to him. All the mailboxes looked the same too, and

46

the bus went too fast for Jonathan to see the names on them. After all, he could only read his own name, and he couldn't read that as fast as the bus was going.

As the children left the bus, they called "Good-by" and "Thanks" to the driver. Jonathan thought they were saying "Good-by, Rus," but this morning Jonathan's friend had called the bus driver, "Wus." Then Jonathan thought of the boy's name. He had said his name was Woland. That is a funny name, thought Jonathan. Woland. Suddenly Jonathan knew that Woland was really Roland. Roland couldn't say *r*. He made everything that began with *r* sound as though it began with a *w*. Mr. Wiley was really Mr. Riley.

Just then the bus stopped, and the driver said, "Here you are, Jonny! Out you go!"

Jonathan wished he did not have to get off right away. He wanted to tell the bus driver about his friend, the milkman, who was also named Mr. Riley, but there wasn't time. The bus had stopped and the door was open. He had to get off. Jonathan just had time to say, "Good-by, Mr. Riley."

"So long, Jonny!" Mr. Riley called back. "You got it right that time. I was beginning to think you talked like Roland Ralston."

Jonathan ran all the way down the lane to his house. He came in calling out, "Mommy! Mommy! I'm home, Mommy!" Cocoa rushed to meet Jonathan. He jumped all over him yelping happily. "Oh, Mommy! Guess what!" said Jonathan.

"What?" said his mother.

"Who do you think drives the bus?" said Jonathan.

"Who?" asked his mother.

"Mr. Riley!" Jonathan replied.

"Whatever do you mean?" said his mother.

"It's true, Mommy, he does," said Jonathan. "His name is Mr. Riley, and he looks just like Mr. Riley, the milkman. And he's nice, Mommy. He's very nice. And he calls me Jonny. Just like Mr. Riley, the milkman."

"Well, I'm glad!" said his mother. "Now tell me how was your first day at school?"

Jonathan knelt down on the floor to pat Cocoa, who was still yelping with joy. "Oh, fine!" he said.

"How was your lunch?" his mother asked.

"Oh, fine!" said Jonathan. "Some girl ran away with my lunch box, and some boy kicked my apple and broke it all up. Then the girl stepped on my sandwich, and my cookies got broken, but I had a good lunch. Molasses gave me one of her sandwiches. It was wonderful. And I didn't drop my bowl of soup."

"Who did you say gave you a sandwich, Jon?" his mother asked.

"Molasses," replied Jonathan.

"Now, Jon!" exclaimed his mother. "No one is ever named Molasses."

"Well, this girl is," said Jonathan. "Anyway, it's something like that. Melissa Molasses!"

49

Jonathan's mother laughed. "Well, Jon!" she said. "I'm glad you had such a good day."

"Yes, and I rode home on the hot seat. Only it isn't hot."

"I see!" said his mother, but she didn't see at all. She was thinking about Melissa Molasses.

Chapter Three

TAFFY AND HIS SHOES

EVERY MORNING Jonathan was eager to ride in the school bus. With his lunch box in his hand, he ran from the house to the mailboxes. Sometimes Cocoa got out the door with him. Then Cocoa waited for the bus, too. While they waited he ran around, smelling here and smelling there. Jonathan knew that he smelled rabbits and other little animals that had been through the tall grass and bushes that grew by the side of the road. After all, Cocoa was a spaniel and spaniels liked to hunt and carry things in their mouth.

Cocoa always forgot about rabbits when the bus arrived. Then he wanted to get on the bus with Jonathan. Sometimes it was hard to get him to go back home. He always watched the bus go without him with sad eyes.

By the end of October, Jonathan knew the names of most of the boys and girls who rode with him on the school bus. He called Mr. Riley, "Rus," just as the other children did. Beside Roland and Melissa, there were Buddy Miller and Roy Stone, who was called Rocky Stone, and Walter Tarr, known as Tar Baby. From the day Jonathan called Melissa "Molasses," she had been called that by all the children who rode on the bus. When Melissa stepped into the bus, the children called out, "Hi, Melissa Molasses!"

Melissa called back, "Hi!" She didn't mind the name Melissa Molasses. She thought it was fun.

One morning Melissa had her little brother with her. She was taking him to kindergarten. His name was Timothy, but he had been called Taffy ever since he was a baby, because his hair was just the color of taffy candy.

Taffy had fallen out of bed and broken his arm, so he did not start kindergarten until the second week in October. He was a little boy who hated shoes. He ran barefooted all summer. When he found out that he had to wear shoes to kindergarten, he raised a terrible fuss.

When his mother took him to the shoe store to buy his shoes for kindergarten, he did not want brown shoes. He did not want black shoes. He did not want red shoes, and he did not want tan shoes. He just did not like any shoes. At last his mother bought a pair of brown shoes for him. She said he would have to wear them.

When the morning came for him to go to kindergarten, Taffy would not put on his shoes. He did not put them on until his sister started out of the door to get the bus. Then Taffy said, "Wait for me, Lissie! Wait for me!"

"Taffy!" said his mother. "For the last time! Put on your shoes!"

Taffy sat down on the floor and put on his new shoes. He did not take time to tie his shoelaces. He ran after Melissa and fell down twice, because he stepped on his shoelaces.

When the children reached the mailbox where the bus would stop, Melissa knelt down and tied Taffy's shoelaces. "Not so tight, Lissie!" said Taffy. "Not so tight!"

"They will fall off if they aren't tight," said Melissa.

"They're too tight," said Taffy.

"They're too loose," said Melissa. "They will fall off."

Soon the bus arrived. When the door opened, Melissa

took hold of her little brother's hand and they stepped into the bus.

"Hello, Taffy!" said Mr. Riley. "Morning, Melissa!"

"Morning, Rus!" said Melissa. Then she said to Taffy, "Say hello to Rus."

"Hi," said Taffy.

"I see you've got a new hat," said Mr. Riley. Taffy was wearing a red hat that was so big it almost covered his eyes.

"He has new shoes too," said Melissa.

"I like my hat," said Taffy.

"Don't you like your shoes?" Mr. Riley asked.

"No," replied Taffy. "Don't like shoes. Like my hat."

As Melissa and Taffy slid into a seat, the children in the bus called out, "Hi, Melissa Molasses!"

"Hi!" Melissa called back.

The first thing Taffy did after he sat down was to kick off his shoes. He wiggled his toes inside his blue socks. Each time the bus stopped and a child got on, he passed by Taffy and kicked his shoes. Each time the shoes were kicked farther away.

A big boy who was sitting behind Melissa said, "What's your little brother's name?"

"Taffy!" replied Melissa.

"My name's Timothy," said Taffy.

"Yes, Timothy," said Melissa, "but we call him, Taffy."

"Oh, molasses taffy!" the boy shouted. Then he called out, so that all the children in the bus could hear, "Melissa Molasses's little brother's name is Molasses Taffy!"

"Molasses Taffy!" the children shouted.

"I am not!" cried Taffy. "I am not!" He poked his underlip out and looked very angry.

"Don't you mind, Taffy," said Melissa. "It just means you're sweet. We're both sweet, like molasses."

"Don't want to be sweet," said Taffy. "Want to be a cowboy."

The big boy called out, "Taffy is a sweet cowboy! Taffy is a sweet cowboy!"

Taffy began to cry. Then he began to scream. He screamed and he yelled as loud as he could. The louder Taffy screamed, the louder the boys and girls shouted, "Molasses Taffy! Molasses Taffy!"

Soon the bus stopped to pick up Jonathan. As the door opened, Mr. Riley left the driver's seat and went back down the aisle of the bus. "This noise has got to stop!" he said. "Stop teasing Taffy. And Taffy, you stop screaming. You come up front with me, on the hot seat." Then Mr. Riley looked down at Taffy, and said, "Where are your shoes?"

Taffy looked down at his feet, and said, "I don't know."

Melissa looked down, and said, "Taffy! Where are your new shoes?"

"I don't know," said Taffy.

While Mr. Riley was leaning over Taffy, he wasn't thinking about Jonathan, who had just got on the bus. He was busy thinking about Taffy's shoes, and he didn't feel something soft and furry brush past his legs. He didn't know there was a dog on the bus until Rocky Stone called out, "Hey, Rus! There's a dog in the bus!"

Jonathan was standing inside the door, calling, "Here, Cocoa! Come here!"

When Mr. Riley heard there was a dog on the bus, he forgot Taffy. He had a very strict rule. "No dogs on the bus."

The children in the back of the bus called out, "He's here, Rus! He's here! Here's the dog!"

Mr. Riley went to the back of the bus. "Come along! Get out of here!" he said to the dog. Cocoa ran, wriggling and yelping, up and down the aisle of the bus. "Out with you!" Mr. Riley kept calling. "Out!"

"Come here, Cocoa!" Jonathan was calling. "Come here!"

Cocoa ran around the children's legs, back and forth. He only stopped once. That was when he went under a seat in the rear of the bus. "Out of there!" Mr. Riley called.

Cocoa ran out from under the seat. He ran down the aisle and out the door. As he dashed past Jonathan, Jonathan saw that Cocoa had something in his mouth, but he couldn't see what it was. Now that the dog was gone, Mr. Riley went to his seat and closed the door. Jonathan looked through the glass in the door, and said, "He's got something! Cocoa's got something in his mouth!"

"Well, he can keep it!" said Mr. Riley. "I have to get this crowd to school."

Having a dog in the bus quieted Taffy. The dog had made the children forget to tease him about his name.

61

Now they were all in the back of the bus, under the seats, looking for his shoes. Only one shoe could be found.

After they had hunted everywhere, Melissa went to Mr. Riley, and said, "We can find only one of Taffy's shoes."

"Oh, it must be there!" said Mr. Riley. "I'll find it when we get to school."

When the bus reached the school, all the children jumped out. All but Melissa and Taffy.

Taffy stood in the aisle in his blue socks. He was holding his one shoe. Melissa took one last look under the seats. "I don't see it!" she said. She looked up at Mr. Riley. "They are Taffy's new shoes."

Suddenly Mr. Riley remembered Jonathan's dog. He remembered that Jonathan had said the dog had something in his mouth. He didn't tell Melissa and Taffy what he was thinking. He just said, "Come along now. Get into school before you're late." He picked up

Taffy. "I'll carry you into kindergarten." So Mr. Riley carried Taffy and Taffy carried his one shoe.

Melissa ran beside Mr. Riley. She said, "Where do you think Taffy's shoe is?"

"I don't know," said Mr. Riley, as Melissa turned to go through the door of the first grade. "But I think I can guess."

When Mr. Riley reached the kindergarten, he said, "Taffy, you will have to get along without your shoes for a while. I want to take this one with me."

"All right!" said Taffy. He liked getting along without his shoes.

After Mr. Riley put Taffy in kindergarten, he went back to his bus. He backed out of the schoolyard and drove to Jonathan's lane. When he got out of the bus, Cocoa came toward him, barking. "Where did you put that shoe?" said Mr. Riley.

Cocoa barked some more.

Mr. Riley began to look under the bushes. Then he

went through the tall grass. Cocoa went with him. He seemed to think that Mr. Riley had come to play with him. He kept jumping up on the bus driver. Then Mr. Riley held Taffy's shoe out to Cocoa. He sniffed the shoe. Mr. Riley said, "Go fetch it, Cocoa!"

Cocoa ran off.

In a few moments he was back. He had Taffy's other shoe in his mouth. It was covered with dirt. Mr. Riley took the shoe from Cocoa's mouth. "What did you do, bury it?" he said.

Mr. Riley patted Cocoa on the head and got back into his bus. He drove back to the school. When he gave the shoes to Taffy, Taffy took them without a word.

"Why, Taffy!" said his teacher. "What do you say to Mr. Riley?"

Taffy said, "Thank you, Mr. Riley," but he didn't sound as though he meant it.

When Mr. Riley left, Taffy said to his teacher, "I don't have to put them on, do I?"

"Of course, you have to put them on," replied his teacher. "You can't go without shoes forever!"

"Why can't I?" said Taffy, as he sat down on the floor to put them on. His teacher didn't reply, so Taffy put on one clean shoe and one dirty shoe. He didn't notice the difference, because shoes were just shoes to him, and he didn't like them anyway.

Chapter Four

THE FORGOTTEN BIRTHDAY CAKE

JONATHAN HAD been looking forward to his sixth birthday. One day he said to his mother, "Mommy, do you think Miss Adams would let me have my birthday party at school?"

"I don't know, Jon," his mother replied. "Why don't you ask her?"

"I could take my birthday cake to school on the bus," said Jonathan.

"I suppose you could," said his mother.

"What about the ice cream?" Jonathan asked.

"Ice cream is delivered to the school every day, for the lunchroom," said his mother. "I'll buy enough ice cream for the first grade."

"Oh, goody!" said Jonathan. "I'll ask Miss Adams if we can have the party."

The next morning, when Jonathan went into his classroom, he went up to Miss Adams.

"Good morning, Jon!" said Miss Adams.

"Good morning, Miss Adams," Jonathan replied. "Can I whisper something to you?"

"What is it?" Miss Adams asked, leaning over.

"My mommy says she will buy the ice cream, if I can have my birthday party here in school," said Jonathan.

"I want to invite all the children in the first grade."

"I think it would be lovely!" said Miss Adams. "When is your birthday?"

"Next Friday," replied Jonathan. "I'll bring a birthday cake too."

"It sounds wonderful!" said Miss Adams.

"You won't tell, will you?" said Jonathan.

"No indeed," replied his teacher.

"It will be a surprise party," said Jonathan.

Miss Adams laughed, and said, "Usually the person having the birthday is the one who is surprised."

Jonathan laughed, too. Then he said, "Yes, but this time everybody is going to be surprised except me."

Melissa heard what Jonathan said, and called out, "What's the surprise?"

"It's a secret," said Miss Adams.

"When will we know?" asked Melissa.

"Next Friday," said Jonathan.

When Jonathan reached home that afternoon, he

rushed into the house and called out, "Mommy! Miss Adams says I can have a birthday party!"

"That's good news!" said his mother. "What kind of birthday cake shall I make?"

"A big one!" Jonathan replied.

"Of course!" his mother said.

"Make that one that tastes like butter," said Jonathan. "And a lot of thick white icing. And red candles."

"Red candles are for Christmas," said his mother. "Pink candles are for birthdays."

"Pink candles are for girls," said Jonathan. "I like red."

"Very well," said his mother. "I'll get red candles. Instead of everyone singing *Happy Birthday,* they can all sing *Jolly Old Saint Nicholas.*"

Jonathan laughed and hung his jacket in the hall closet.

The day before Jonathan's birthday, his mother made the cake. When he came home, it was standing on the kitchen table. It was covered all over with creamy white icing, and it looked beautiful. It was the biggest birthday cake Jonathan had ever seen. "Did you get red candles, Mommy?" Jonathan asked.

"Yes, I have six of them," his mother replied.

"When do we put them on the cake?" said Jonathan.

"You had better carry them in your lunch box," said his mother. "Then you can put them on the cake just before the party."

"We're going to have the party at lunchtime," said Jonathan.

"I'm going to put the cake in this hatbox," said his mother, holding up a round hatbox. "You'll have to carry it carefully, Jon."

"I'll carry it carefully, all right," said Jonathan. "I don't want anything to happen to my birthday cake."

The following morning Jonathan's cake was packed away in the hatbox. His mother packed it very carefully. It was covered with wax paper, and rolls of wax paper kept the sides of the cake from rubbing against the box. The lid was tied down with a strong cord. "I'll carry it to the bus for you, Jon," said his mother.

"Oh no, Mommy! I can carry it," said Jonathan. "I want to carry it myself."

"But you have your lunch box to carry and your books," said his mother.

"I'll carry my books on my back," said Jonathan. "And I have two hands!"

"You can't carry the cake box by the string," said his mother. "You'll need both hands."

"Well, I can do it!" said Jonathan, as he put on his jacket. "I'll show you." When Jonathan picked up the box, his arms were full.

"Now how are you going to carry your lunch box?" his mother asked.

"On top," said Jonathan.

"All right," said his mother, "but if you drop the cake, you'll have to have your party with a broken birthday cake."

"I won't drop it," said Jonathan, as he went out the door. "I'll walk slowly."

Cocoa ran out, but Jonathan's mother called him back. "You stay here, Cocoa," she said. "Jon has enough to take care of."

Jonathan couldn't see where he was walking very well. Once he tripped over a stone in the road, but he caught himself and didn't drop anything. By the time he reached the mailboxes, the birthday cake seemed heavier than it had when he started out. It was too heavy to hold until the bus arrived.

Jonathan looked around for a place to rest the box. He didn't want to put it on the ground. A bug might get into it. He decided that the best place would be right on top of the mailboxes. Mr. Tattersall, who was farming the Masons' land, had his mailbox right beside

Jonathan's. It leaned toward it in a friendly kind of way. Together the two mailboxes made a big enough shelf to hold the birthday cake. Jonathan put it down very carefully. Then he felt it to see if it was steady. He didn't want anything to happen to that cake.

Jonathan stood waiting for the bus with his lunch box in his hand. He kicked the fallen leaves that lay beside the road. Then he looked up at the trees. Their black branches were almost bare against the blue sky. He watched a great flock of birds flying south. He knew that they were getting away from the cold winter, which would soon come.

Looking up, Jonathan felt the sun on his face. The sun was still warm, but the morning air was chilly. He sniffed the air. For weeks it had been filled with the odor of burning leaves. He looked down at the leaves. He saw red leaves, pink leaves, purple leaves, brown leaves, and leaves every color of yellow, from pale lemon to deep gold. Jonathan thought they were beautiful. He began to pick up the ones he thought were the prettiest. As he picked them up, he walked up the road. Here he found a cherry-colored one, there an orange one. Soon he had a large bunch of beautiful leaves. He looked at them carefully and decided to take them to school. Perhaps Miss Adams would like to stick them on the blackboard.

Jonathan was so busy selecting leaves that he forgot to think about the bus. He had walked quite a way from his own mailbox. Suddenly, as if by magic, the school bus stopped beside him.

When the door opened, Mr. Riley called out, "Hi, Jonny! Were you walking to meet me this morning?"

Jonathan stepped into the bus. "Hi, Rus!" he said. Then he held up the bunch of brightly colored leaves. "Look! Aren't they pretty?"

"Sure are!" said Rus, as he closed the door.

Mr. Riley stepped on the gas, and the school bus bounced off. Jonathan sat down without thinking of

his birthday cake. He didn't think of it until Melissa Molasses, who was sitting on the hot seat, said, "Jonny, it's Friday! You said you would tell me your secret on Friday. What's the secret?"

Jonathan jumped up as though he had suddenly sat on a bumblebee. "Oh, Rus!" he cried out, as he rushed up the aisle of the bus. "Rus! I have to go back! I left my birthday cake on the mailbox."

"We can't go back now," said Mr. Riley. "If I go back now, the whole busload will be late for school."

"But it's for my birthday party," said Jonathan.

"I'll go back and get it after I get this crowd to school," said Mr. Riley.

"Where is the birthday party going to be?" asked Melissa.

"At school," replied Jonathan.

"For everybody?" exclaimed Melissa.

"For everybody in our room," said Jonathan.

"You mean with ice cream?" said Melissa.

81

"Yepper!" replied Jonathan. He was still standing beside Mr. Riley. "You won't forget to go back and get my birthday cake, will you, Rus?" he said.

"I won't forget," replied Mr. Riley.

"It's on top of the mailboxes," said Jonathan. "It's in one of my mommy's hatboxes."

"Okay!" said Rus.

"You'll have to carry it carefully," said Jonathan, "so it doesn't break."

"Okay, okay!" said Rus. "Sit down and stop pestering me."

By the time the bus reached the school, everyone knew that Jonathan was having a birthday party in the first grade. Everyone also knew that he had left his birthday cake sitting on top of the mailboxes at the end of the lane. As they got off the bus, the whole first grade reminded Mr. Riley to go back and get the birthday cake.

"I'll get it!" he replied.

When the bus was empty, Mr. Riley turned it around and started back. "Just imagine!" he said to himself. "Imagine forgetting your birthday cake!"

Chapter Five

WHO'S GOT THE CAKE?

WHILE MR. RILEY was driving the school bus back over the country roads, the mailman was driving from mailbox to mailbox. He stopped beside a mailbox, opened up the little door, placed the letters or packages, and sometimes magazines and newspapers, inside. Sometimes the mailman found letters inside the mailbox waiting for him. These he picked up and took with him to the post office. Sometimes there were even packages waiting for him.

The mailman's name was Joe Davis, and he tried very hard to help everybody. He knew that it was hard at times for people who lived out in the country to get to the post office in town.

Not long after the school bus had picked up Jonathan, the mailman stopped to leave some letters for Jonathan's father in the Masons' mailbox. When he stopped his car, he was surprised to find a large round hatbox sitting on top of the mailboxes. Mr. Davis looked at it carefully. It looked like a brand-new hatbox to him. It had the name of the town's best hat store right on the lid.

Mr. Davis turned the box all around. On one side he saw Jonathan's mother's name—Mrs. David Mason. He pushed his hat back and scratched his head. He was puzzled. He wondered what he was supposed to do with this hatbox.

After a few moments, he decided to take it with him. He guessed that Mrs. Mason wanted the hat to go back to the hat shop. He picked it up and placed it on the front seat of his car.

Mr. Davis drove from mailbox to mailbox along the country roads. He passed fields where the corn had been cut down. It was piled in neat piles shaped like Indian wigwams, called corn shocks. Here and there a big yellow pumpkin lay against the corn shocks. Mr. Davis looked at the last leaves dropping from the trees. He passed apple orchards and called out to the farmers who were gathering the last of the apples. "Morning, Will!" "Morning, Tom!" He knew everybody and everybody knew him.

When Mr. Davis stopped to leave the mail at Mrs. Trimbull's, she was standing beside the mailbox with a

letter in her hand. "Morning, Mrs. Trimbull!" said the mailman, as he pulled up beside her. "Think I've got a letter for you this morning."

"Well, I've got one for you," said Mrs. Trimbull. "It's a letter to my grandson. He's in the army now."

"He'll be glad to get that," said Mr. Davis, taking the letter from her. He looked through the letters in his pouch, and muttered, "Now I was sure I had a letter for you. Where did that letter get to?"

Mr. Davis looked on the seat of the car. Then he moved the hatbox and there, behind it, was a bundle of letters. "Ah! There's your letter! Right on top of this bundle. Couldn't see it for this hatbox."

Mr. Davis handed the letter to Mrs. Trimbull, and said, "People do funny things 'round here! Those new people just moved here from a big city, Mason's the name. Well, she left this hatbox sitting right on top of the mailboxes. I guess she thought I'd drop it off at the hat shop. I brought it along."

"I don't know what we'd do without you, Joe," said Mrs. Trimbull.

"Oh, I'm glad to do these little things," replied Mr. Davis. "I go right past the shop."

"Well, it's good of you, Joe," said Mrs. Trimbull, looking up the road. She looked puzzled, then she said, "Now why do you suppose Rus Riley is driving his school bus back this way? He went past here with the children over a half-hour ago."

The mailman looked up the road. Sure enough! Rus Riley was driving toward them. As he neared the mailman's car, Mr. Riley slowed down. He shifted his gears, but he didn't quite stop. As he went by, he called out the window, "I have to go back for a birthday cake. First grader forgot his birthday cake."

Mr. Davis and Mrs. Trimbull both laughed. "I don't know what we'd do without Rus either," said Mrs. Trimbull. "He drove my grandson to school when he was little." The mailman and Mrs. Trimbull watched the school bus until it disappeared.

When the school bus arrived at the Masons' mailbox, the hatbox, of course, was gone. "Now what!" Mr. Riley said aloud. Just as Mr. Davis had done, Mr. Riley pushed his hat back and scratched his head. Then he turned the bus into the lane and drove up it to the Masons' house.

Mr. Riley got out of the bus and rang the front door-bell. When Jonathan's mother opened the door, she was surprised to see him and the big yellow school bus. "Why, Mr. Riley!" she exclaimed. "What's the matter?"

"It's that birthday cake!" said Mr. Riley. "Jonny forgot it."

"But he took it with him," said Mrs. Mason.

"Yes, I know, but he left it on top of the mailboxes," said Mr. Riley.

"He left it on top of the mailboxes!" exclaimed Jonathan's mother.

"That's right!" said Mr. Riley. "I came back for it, but it's gone."

"Oh, how awful!" said Mrs. Mason. "Who do you suppose took it?"

"I don't know," said Mr. Riley. "Could have been Joe when he left the mail, but I spoke to him on my way out. He didn't say anything to me."

"I'll telephone the post office," said Mrs. Mason. "Maybe he's there."

Mrs. Mason called the post office while Mr. Riley waited in the hall. When she heard a voice on the other end of the telephone, she said, "Has Joe Davis come in?"

"No, ma'am!" was the reply. "Joe won't be in until around three o'clock."

"Thank you," said Jonathan's mother, and she hung

up the telephone. She came back to Mr. Riley. "Joe Davis won't be back at the post office until three o'clock. I can't bake another cake, and I can't go into town to buy one, because my husband has our car."

"I guess the first grade is not paying much attention to Miss Adams this morning," said Mr. Riley. "They are all watching for the birthday cake."

"Isn't it dreadful?" said Mrs. Mason. "It was good of you to come all the way out here, Mr. Riley."

"Wish there was something I could do about it," said Mr. Riley. "I could take you in to town, but I couldn't bring you back, so that wouldn't do any good."

Suddenly an idea came to Mrs. Mason. "Oh, Mr. Riley!" she said. "Do you suppose you could buy a birthday cake for me at the bakery in town? Could you take it to the school?"

"I don't see why not!" said Mr. Riley.

"Oh, Mr. Riley! That's wonderful!" said Mrs.

Mason. "I can't bear to have the children disappointed."

"Be a shame!" said Mr. Riley.

Mrs. Mason gave Mr. Riley the money to pay for the birthday cake. He put it in his pocket, and said, "Don't worry about it. I'll get a birthday cake."

Mr. Riley got into the bus and drove off.

In the meantime, the mailman was driving over the country roads, leaving the mail in the mailboxes.

After some time, he picked up the hatbox to see if any

letters had got under the box. When he picked it up, he thought to himself, This is a very heavy hat. He began to wonder whether it was a hat after all.

Mr. Davis decided to look inside the box. He untied the string. Then he lifted the lid. He looked down into a lot of wax paper. He lifted the wax paper, and there he saw the birthday cake.

Mr. Davis was very surprised. After thinking for a few minutes, he decided that he had better get the cake back to the place where he had found it. He drove back across country. This was the shortest way to Jonathan's mailbox. He decided that whoever had left the cake on top of the mailboxes did not wish the mailman to take it. Mr. Davis hoped that he had not done any harm. Like Melissa Molasses, on the first day Jonathan had gone to school, Mr. Davis had just meant to be helpful.

"A birthday cake!" Mr. Davis said to himself. "Imagine leaving a birthday cake on top of a mailbox!"

Suddenly Mr. Davis remembered that Rus Riley had called out something about a birthday cake to him. He thought a minute longer. Then he recalled what the bus driver had said. "A first grader forgot his birthday cake."

"Oh, my!" Mr. Davis said aloud. "I'm going the wrong way with this birthday cake. I have to take this to the first grade."

Mr. Davis turned around and went back to where he had been when he discovered that he had a birthday cake on the front seat of his car. In about a half-hour he would be passing the school, and he would deliver the cake to the first grade. He knew that they would be glad to see it for he guessed there was to be a party.

The school bus flew along the main road to town. When Mr. Riley reached the center of town, he ran his bus into his garage and walked to the bakery shop on the main street.

When Mr. Riley opened the door, the girl behind the counter said, "Hello, Rus, what can I do for you?"

"You can sell me a birthday cake," said Mr. Riley. "A big one! And don't tell me you haven't got one."

"Well, you're lucky!" said the girl. "I do have one."

While the girl was packing the cake in a box, she said, "Who's having a birthday party?"

"Little fellow in the first grade," said Mr. Riley. "He started out with one this morning, but he left it on his mailbox and it disappeared."

"Oh, my!" said the girl. "That first grader will be glad to see you when you walk in with this cake."

97

Mr. Riley picked up the box and paid for the cake. Then he went back to his garage, got into his own car, and drove to the school.

When Mr. Riley reached the school, he opened a side door that led into a long hall. As he entered the hall, he saw a door open on the opposite side of the school. A man stepped into the other end of the hall. As the man came toward Mr. Riley, the bus driver saw that he was also carrying a box. As he came nearer, Mr. Riley saw that the man was Joe Davis, the mailman.

When the mailman recognized his friend, Rus Riley, he called out, "Hello, Rus! What have you got there?"

"A birthday cake," replied Mr. Riley. "What have you got?"

"A birthday cake!" said Mr. Davis. "I found it on top of the mailbox. Where did yours come from?"

"From the bakery," said Mr. Riley. "I thought that one was lost." He looked from one box to the other.

"Well!" he said. "I guess the first grade will have enough birthday cake."

The mailman and the bus driver went to the door of the first grade. It was just twelve o'clock. Miss Adams and all the children looked at the two men standing in the doorway, each holding a large box. "Here is Jonny's birthday cake," said Mr. Riley. "Only now it is birthday *cakes.*"

"Oh, do stay and join the party!" said Miss Adams.

"Thanks!" said the bus driver and the mailman in a chorus.

So Mr. Davis and Mr. Riley stayed for Jonathan's birthday party and they all ate cake, not once, but twice. It was the first time Jonathan had had two birthday cakes. Everybody in the first grade thought it was a very good idea.

Chapter Six

THE PUMPKIN PEOPLE

As the end of October drew near, the Pumpkin People appeared. Jonathan had never seen Pumpkin People before. He had only seen pumpkin heads.

At Halloween his father had always bought a big

pumpkin. Then he cut the top off and scooped out the inside. When only the thick shell remained, he cut out the eyes and the nose and a big wide mouth. He called it a jack-o'-lantern.

Jonathan always helped. His father had to do the cutting, but Jonathan picked up bits of pumpkin, and he always put the candle inside the pumpkin shell. When it was finished, he carried it to the window sill in his bedroom. At night his father lit the candle and the jack-o'-lantern had grinned out into the darkness.

Jonathan loved to lie in bed with no light in the room except the light from his jack-o'-lantern. It made an orange glow on the curtains. He always fell asleep while the candle was burning. His mother came in later and snuffed it out.

The first time Jonathan saw the Pumpkin People, he was riding to school on the bus. He was sitting on the hot seat beside Mr. Riley, and he was looking out the window. Suddenly he saw, what appeared to be, a little dwarf. It was sitting on a small chair that was placed beside the front door of a farmhouse. It was not far from the road. Jonathan could see it plainly.

"Oh, look!" cried Jonathan, pointing with his finger. "Look, Rus!"

Mr. Riley was so surprised that he slowed down the bus. "What is it?" he asked.

"Over there," said Jonathan, "sitting on that chair! It has a jack-o'-lantern head, and it's all dressed up."

Mr. Riley looked, and said, "Oh, that's one of the Pumpkin People. You'll see more of them."

Sure enough! Not much farther on, Jonathan called out, "There are three more Pumpkin People."

"Yes," said Mr. Riley, "a whole family, sitting on chairs. Mr. and Mrs. Pumpkin and Peter Pumpkin."

"What are they made of?" asked Jonathan.

"Oh, you stuff an old suit to make Mr. Pumpkin and an old dress for Mrs. Pumpkin and a little boy's suit for Peter Pumpkin."

102

"They have hats on, too," said Jonathan.

"Mrs. Pumpkin is wearing a scarf over her head, I think," said Mr. Riley.

"What do people stuff them with?" asked Jonathan.

"Well, often as not, it's hay or just old newspapers," said Mr. Riley.

When Jonathan reached home, he rushed into the house calling out, "Mommy, Mommy! The Pumpkin People are out!"

"Who is out, Jon?" his mother asked.

"The Pumpkin People," said Jonathan.

"Now who are the Pumpkin People?" said Mrs. Mason.

Jonathan told his mother about the Pumpkin People he had seen. When he finished, he said, "Do you think Daddy will make one for us, instead of just a jack-o'-lantern?"

"If we can find some clothes, perhaps he will," said his mother. "Let's look."

"Yes, let's!" said Jonathan.

"We'll look in the chest where we keep old costumes," said his mother.

Mrs. Mason and Jonathan went to a closet, and his mother pulled out a wooden chest. When she lifted the lid, there on the top of the pile was a Santa Claus suit. Jonathan had worn it last year at his kindergarten Christmas party.

"Well," said his mother, "that won't do!"

"No!" said Jonathan. "That won't do! We don't want a Santa Claus Pumpkin Man."

His mother laid the Santa Claus suit on the floor. Next in the chest there was a Scottish kilt and jacket. Mrs. Mason picked them up, and said, "I don't think the Pumpkin People are Scottish."

"I didn't see any Scottish ones," said Jonathan.

His mother laid the kilt and jacket on top of the Santa Claus costume. Now she uncovered a clown suit. "How about this clown suit?" she asked.

"No, that won't do," said Jonathan. "The Pumpkin People look like real people."

Mrs. Mason lifted up the clown suit. Underneath there were a pair of faded blue jeans of Jonathan's, a plaid shirt, a bandanna handkerchief, and an old felt hat. "That's it! That's it!" Jonathan shouted. "My cowboy suit!"

"Oh!" said his mother. "I didn't know that Mr. Pumpkin was to be a cowboy."

"He won't be a cowboy," said Jonathan. "'Cause he won't wear a belt with two guns. But he will look like a real Pumpkin Man in those clothes."

Mrs. Mason lifted the blue jeans and the plaid shirt out of the chest. Jonathan picked up the brightly colored bandanna handkerchief and the old felt hat. "Now we have to get a nice pumpkin for the head."

"That will be easy," said his mother. "Mr. Tattersall has a lot of pumpkins. He gathered them all out of his field. He told me to help myself."

"Can we go now and get one?" Jonathan asked.

"We might as well," his mother replied.

Jonathan and his mother put on their coats. Then they walked up the lane until they came to Mr. Tattersall's house. They found Mr. Tattersall burning a pile of leaves. When he saw them, he called out, "How do, Mrs. Mason! How do, Jonathan!" Mr. Tattersall was the only person who called Jonathan by his real name.

"Hello, Mr. Tattersall!" said Jonathan.

"How are you, Mr. Tattersall?" Mrs. Mason asked.

"Can't complain," said Mr. Tattersall.

"I'm going to make a Pumpkin Person," said Jonathan. "A Mr. Pumpkin."

"Don't say!" said Mr. Tattersall.

"We thought we might find a nice pumpkin for the pumpkin gentleman's head," said Jonathan's mother.

"Wouldn't be surprised!" said Mr. Tattersall. "Come look 'em over."

Mr. Tattersall led Jonathan and his mother to a large

pile of bright golden pumpkins. The pile was near the house. He picked up a long narrow pumpkin. "How's this?" he asked.

Jonathan looked at the pumpkin. Then he looked up at his mother.

"What do you think, Jon?" his mother asked.

"It's a nice pumpkin," said Jonathan, "but I think Mr. Pumpkin would look sad with such a long face."

Mr. Tattersall picked up another pumpkin. This one was swollen on one side. He looked at it carefully. Jonathan hoped he would not have to take this one. He didn't want his pumpkin man to look as though he had a terrible toothache.

Jonathan gave a sigh of relief when Mr. Tattersall put it back on the pile, saying, "Guess that won't do, either." Jonathan watched as Mr. Tattersall went through the pile of pumpkins. He kept saying, "That's too big." "That's too little." At last, he picked up a perfectly round pumpkin. It was just the right size and just the right shape. "How's this?" he asked, holding it up.

"That's a good one!" Jonathan exclaimed.

"That will make a jolly pumpkin gentleman," said his mother.

Mr. Tattersall put the pumpkin into Jonathan's arms. "Thank you, Mr. Tattersall," said Jonathan.

Jonathan carried the pumpkin home. On the way he said to his mother, "I can't wait to put Mr. Pumpkin together."

That evening Jonathan sat on the kitchen floor and stuffed old newspapers into the legs of his old blue jeans. His mother had sewed up the bottoms of the trouser legs, so that the newspaper would not fall through. Now she was busy sewing up the ends of the shirt sleeves. While Jonathan stuffed the legs of the jeans, his father made the jack-o'-lantern. He worked at the kitchen table.

Jonathan was surprised to find that he needed a great

deal of newspaper to stuff the legs. He stuffed and stuffed. When he had the legs full of newspaper, his mother sewed the plaid shirt to the blue jeans. Jonathan sat on the floor looking at the limp shirt. "That shirt is going to take an awful lot of newspaper," he said. "I wish I had something big to put inside it."

"You should put a pillow in the shirt," said Jonathan's father.

"Oh, a pillow would be good!" said Jonathan.

"I think I have an old pillow," said Jonathan's mother.

Mrs. Mason went off to look for the pillow while Jonathan stuffed newspaper into the sleeves of the shirt. When his mother returned, she had an old pillow in her hand. "Here it is," she said. "The cover isn't very strong, but that won't make any difference. No one is going to get rough with Mr. Pumpkin."

"You mean, Mr. Pumpkin doesn't get into fights?" asked Jonathan's father, laughing.

109

"Oh, no!" said Jonathan's mother. "Mr. Pumpkin is a gentleman."

"He doesn't look like one," said Mr. Mason. Jonathan and his father and mother laughed.

Mr. Pumpkin was finished quickly now. When his shirt was buttoned over the pillow, he was quite a plump little man.

Jonathan left him, propped against the wall, and went to watch his father. Mr. Mason was just finishing Mr. Pumpkin's head. "Oh, he looks very happy!" said Jonathan.

"That's because I'm such a good dentist," said his father, as he cut out a good square tooth.

"How will you fasten the head to the body?" Jonathan asked.

"That's a good question," said his father. "I haven't thought of that." After a few minutes, he said, "I guess the thing to do is to put a stick up his back and put the head on the stick."

"That sounds like a good idea," said Jonathan's mother.

Mr. Mason found a good, strong stick in the wood-bin. He nailed one end to a small crosspiece of wood, and said, "This will help the head stay straight."

Jonathan and his mother watched while Mr. Mason pushed the stick down, inside the shirt, back of the pillow. As he did so, he said, "There you are, old boy! Now you have a good backbone." Mr. Mason thought he heard a sound, like something being torn, as he pushed the stick down, but he thought nothing of it. When Mr. Pumpkin's head was settled on his shoulders, Jonathan was delighted with him.

"Now that he's finished," said his father, "where do we put him?"

"On my little chair outside," said Jonathan.

Jonathan picked up his chair, and his father picked up Mr. Pumpkin. Outside Jonathan looked around, and said, "Nobody will see Mr. Pumpkin but us and maybe Mr. Tattersall, if he comes along. No cars go by."

"That's true," said his father.

"There's nothing for Mr. Pumpkin to see, and nobody to see Mr. Pumpkin," said Jonathan.

"How about putting him out by the mailboxes?" his father said.

"Oh, that's a good idea!" said Jonathan. "That's a wonderful idea!"

Jonathan carried the chair down the lane to the mailboxes, and Mr. Mason carried Mr. Pumpkin. They placed him on the opposite side of the lane from the mailboxes, in front of a large bush. "Now everybody can see him," said Jonathan.

"And he won't miss anything," said his father, with a chuckle.

The following morning, when he reached the mailboxes to wait for the bus, Jonathan looked Mr. Pumpkin over carefully. He suddenly decided that it would be nice to take Mr. Pumpkin to school. By the time the bus arrived, he had thought of a way to carry Mr. Pumpkin. When the door opened, he had his right arm around Mr. Pumpkin's middle while his left hand held Mr. Pumpkin's head.

"Hi, Jonny!" Mr. Riley called out. "What's all that?"

"It's a Pumpkin Person," Jonathan replied. "I'm going to take him to school."

"Certainly got your hands full," said Mr. Riley. "Here, let me help you."

Mr. Riley left his wheel and came to the door. As he reached out and took the armload from Jonathan, Jonathan said, "Be careful his head doesn't fall off."

"He better not lose his head in this bus," said Mr. Riley.

"Oh, look!" cried the children, as Mr. Riley placed the Pumpkin Man on a seat. A lot of children stood up to see Mr. Pumpkin.

"He's got a fat tummy," said Tar Baby.

"He sure has!" said Rocky Stone, who was sitting across the aisle. "What's he made of?"

Before Jonathan could reply, Rocky punched Mr. Pumpkin right in his middle. The buttons flew off Mr. Pumpkin's shirt. There was the sound of a tear. Then feathers flew out into the air. "Now look!" Jonathan cried. "Look what you did!"

"Feathers!" the children cried. "Feathers!"

"Stop that carrying on!" Mr. Riley called out. "Leave that Pumpkin Man alone."

Just then the bus went over a bump. Mr. Pumpkin bounced in his seat and more feathers flew out. They floated through the bus. They caught on the girls' hair. They stuck to the boys' and girls' woolly caps. A feather landed on a candy apple that Taffy was carrying on a stick. He tried to pull it off with his mittens on, and his mittens stuck to the apple, too.

The bus bumped again. More feathers rose from Mr.

Pumpkin. Taffy waved the feathers away, but a lot of them stuck to his sticky mittens. Once again he tried to pull the feather off his apple, but more feathers from his mittens stuck to the apple instead.

By the time the bus reached the school, everyone had feathers. Even Mr. Riley had a feather on his ear. "Jonny!" said Mr. Riley, when the bus stopped. "You better not take that pumpkin fellow into school. Miss Adams won't be glad to have those feathers in her room. You better let me take him back to your place."

"All right," said Jonathan. "Try not to bump him so much."

"I'll try," said Mr. Riley.

As Jonathan stepped out of the bus, he turned back and said, "Rus! Be careful of his head."

"Don't worry!" Mr. Riley replied.

"You'll sit him on the chair, won't you?"

"Okay! I'll sit him on the chair," Mr. Riley called back.

When Jonathan returned from school, he found Mr. Pumpkin sitting on the chair. He was much thinner than he had been when they had left for school in the morning. Jonathan pulled Mr. Pumpkin's shirt together, straightened his hat, and ran up the road to his house.

Just before dark Jonathan looked out the window. It had begun to rain. He thought of Mr. Pumpkin sitting out by the road in the rain. He could not bear to think of him out there getting all wet.

Jonathan went to the coat closet and put on his yellow rubber coat. Then he put on his yellow rubber hat and his yellow rubber boots. He went out of the house and down the lane to the mailboxes. He picked up Mr. Pumpkin and carried him back to the house. He left a trail of feathers all the way.

Mrs. Mason opened the door just as Jonathan reached it. "What's the matter, Jon?" she asked.

118

"I'm bringing Mr. Pumpkin in out of the rain," he replied.

Mrs. Mason saw the feathers, and she cried, "Oh, don't bring any feathers in!"

"But I can't get Mr. Pumpkin away from his feathers," said Jonathan. "He's all feathery!"

"Put him in the woodshed," said his mother.

Jonathan took Mr. Pumpkin to the woodshed. He propped him against the woodpile. Mr. Pumpkin looked very bedraggled.

Jonathan decided that if he could not have all of Mr. Pumpkin in the house, he would have some of him. He lifted Mr. Pumpkin's head off his body and carried it up to his bedroom. He put it on the window sill. Then he placed a candle inside and soon a jolly jack-o'-lantern was shining in the window of Jonathan's room. He seemed to be laughing at the rain.

The next morning it was still pouring. On the way

to school Jonathan watched through the streaming windows of the bus for the Pumpkin People. He wondered whether they would still be sitting on their chairs. When the bus reached the house where the three Pumpkin People sat, Jonathan called out, "Hey, Rus! Look, Rus! The Pumpkin People are sitting under a big umbrella."

"What do you know!" said Mr. Riley. "A big red umbrella."

Chapter Seven

THE CHRISTMAS TREE

BY THE middle of December, the outside world lay
covered with snow. With each snowfall, the snowplows appeared. They traveled over the country roads,
pushing the snow aside. They plowed the main roads
first. Then they plowed the lanes.

Sometimes the lane where Jonathan's house stood didn't get plowed out for several days after a storm. Then Jonathan would have to put on his rubber boots instead of his galoshes and walk out to the road through the deep snow. If there had been a fresh fall of snow during the night, the mailbox would look like a big cake, topped with thick white icing.

More and more parcels appeared in the Masons' mailbox. The pile of letters was larger every day, for Christmas would soon be here. The school bus, driving over the snow-covered roads, picked up rosy-cheeked children. Their eyes grew brighter every day as they chattered about Christmas.

In school the children were making ornaments to hang on the Christmas tree. They made long strings of colored-paper rings, little paper baskets to hold candies, gold and silver stars, and crescent moons. They strung long strings of popcorn and long strings of cranberries.

122

The pile of ornaments for the first grade's Christmas tree grew larger every day.

One morning, the week before Christmas, Jonathan was sitting on the hot seat beside Mr. Riley. "Rus," said Jonathan, "Miss Adams says you're going to get us a Christmas tree."

"That's right!" replied Mr. Riley.

"Where will you get it?" asked Jonathan.

"Out in the woods," replied Mr. Riley.

"You mean, you're going to chop it down?" said Jonathan.

"That's right," said Mr. Riley. "Every year I go out and chop down a tree for Miss Adams' first grade."

"I'd like to see that!" said Jonathan. "Can I go with you?"

Melissa Molasses, who was sitting on the first seat behind Mr. Riley, said, "Can I go, too, Rus?"

"I guess so," said Mr. Riley. "Guess I might as well take the whole first grade."

"Do you mean it, Rus!" Melissa exclaimed.

"Sure!" Mr. Riley replied.

Melissa turned around and called out to the other children, "Rus is going to take us to cut down a Christmas tree!"

This happy news was repeated by the other children and ran all through the bus. "Rus is going to take us to cut down a Christmas tree."

"Will we go in the bus?" Jonathan asked Mr. Riley.

"That's right!" said Mr. Riley. "I have to bring the tree back to the school in the bus."

Melissa called out again, "We're going in the bus to get the Christmas tree." There were squeals of joy from the children.

"When will we go?" Jonathan asked Mr. Riley.

"After school on Monday," said Mr. Riley. "We'll take Miss Adams along."

Melissa turned around again. "We're going after

school on Monday," she shouted. More squeals and happy yells greeted this latest news.

On Monday the children could hardly wait until school was over. When the bell rang, they were already bundled up in their sweaters, snowpants, jackets, hoods, caps, earmuffs, scarves, boots, and mittens. School was over at last, and they could go to the woods to get the Christmas tree.

They piled into the bus, shouting, "Hi, Rus! We're going to get the Christmas tree!"

"That's right!" Mr. Riley replied.

"We're going to get a big one, aren't we?" said Jonathan.

"To reach to the ceiling," said Melissa.

"We're going to stand it in the corner of the first grade, aren't we, Miss Adams?" said Rocky, as he climbed onto the hot seat.

"Yes, we are," Miss Adams replied.

127

Jonathan got into the seat right behind Mr. Riley. When Mr. Riley took his place at the wheel, Jonathan said, "Rus, where are we going to get the Christmas tree?"

"Up on Dobson's Ridge, where there's a big growth of evergreen trees," Mr. Riley replied. "We'll find a good Christmas tree there."

Jonathan thought about this. In a few minutes, he said, "Rus, do the Christmas trees belong to Mr. Dobson?"

"That's right!" Mr. Riley replied. "He has hundreds of them."

"Won't we get arrested if we take one of Mr. Dobson's Christmas trees?" Jonathan asked.

"Don't you worry, Jonny!" said Mr. Riley. "We aren't going to steal the tree. Mr. Dobson lets us cut one down every year."

"Oh! That's nice of Mr. Dobson!" said Jonathan, with a sigh of relief.

The bus bounced along the country roads. There was no "stop and go" as there was when the children were being dropped off at the end of the day. It wasn't long before Mr. Riley turned into a road that led through a grove of evergreen trees. They were all spruce trees, and there were hundreds of them—big trees, little trees, medium-sized trees. Snow clung to their branches. Jonathan had never seen so many Christmas trees in one place.

Mr. Riley drove very slowly along the narrow road. Finally he stopped. He opened the door and stepped out into the smooth snow. The children and Miss Adams followed him. "Now!" said Mr. Riley. "Let's pick out the Christmas tree."

"A big one! A big one!" the children cried. "We want a big one!" The children tramped around in the snow, making big footprints.

"Here's a big one!" Melissa called out, pointing to a giant tree.

"We couldn't get that tree inside the school," said Mr. Riley.

"Here's one! Here's one!" Jonathan called out, pointing to one almost as big.

"Too big, Jonny!" said Mr. Riley. "Couldn't get that inside of the bus."

"What about this one?" Rocky called out, pointing to a much smaller tree.

"That's more like it!" said Mr. Riley.

"It's too little!" the children cried. "It's too little!"

"No, that's about right," said Mr. Riley.

"Ah, it's too little!" said Melissa, looking up into the branches. "Anyway," she added, "it has a bird's nest in it. We can't chop it down if it has a bird's nest in it, can we, Miss Adams? The birds would come back next spring and their house would be gone."

"That's right!" the children sang out.

"We can't cut that one down, can we, Miss Adams?" asked Jonathan.

"No, no!" said Miss Adams. "Let's pick another one."

"A big one," the children called out once more.

"One that will reach to the ceiling," said Melissa.

They all tramped around some more in the snow, looking up at the trees. The more they looked, the harder it was to decide upon the right one. Before long everyone had a favorite tree. They were all big ones.

"Now look here!" said Mr. Riley. "These trees that you want are all too big. Not one of them would go inside the bus."

Soon the children were calling out, "Here's a little one, Rus. Here's a little one!" But it was always a big tree.

Finally Mr. Riley said, "Now I am going to pick out a tree and cut it down. You children can watch. We can't stay here all night."

Mr. Riley walked up to a tree. The children watched him while he walked all around the tree. Then he stood off and looked at it. He picked up his ax. "Stand back!" he called out. "Stand back, all of you."

The children gathered around Miss Adams, like baby chicks around a mother hen. Mr. Riley raised his ax. Jonathan called out, "Don't let him, Miss Adams! It's too little!"

"We want a big one!" Melissa called out.

Mr. Riley made believe he did not hear them. He hacked at the trunk of the tree. The chips flew and a shower of snow fell from the dark green branches. The sound of the ax echoed through the Ridge.

The children were silent now as they watched Rus chopping down the tree; their faces were not gay. Such a little Christmas tree, was what they were thinking.

When the tree fell, the children's voices returned. "It's too little," they grumbled. "It won't reach the ceiling. We want a big one."

"This is a big one," said Mr. Riley, as he tied a rope around the branches to keep them from breaking.

132

When the tree was well tied, he dragged it across the snow to the back of the bus. "I'll leave it here," he said to Miss Adams, "while I go inside and open the rear door."

In a moment the door was open, and Mr. Riley jumped down. "I'll help you put it in," said Miss Adams.

"Thanks!" said Mr. Riley. "The trunk goes in first."

Most of the children were inside the bus now, watching for the Christmas tree. When the trunk appeared, they shouted, "Here it comes! Here it comes! Here comes the Christmas tree!" As more and more of the tree filled the aisle, the children climbed onto the seats. The farther up the aisle the tree came, the happier their faces grew. When at last the rear door was locked, the Christmas tree reached from the front of the bus to the back. The children were all surprised.

"See!" said Mr. Riley. "Didn't I tell you!"

Mr. Riley backed the bus out of the evergreen grove, and soon the children were on their way to their homes. It was getting dark. Mr. Riley turned on the lights. The headlights of the bus made a golden path on the snow-covered road.

In the warmth of the bus, the Christmas tree began to give out the pungent odor of spruce. "Smells like Christmas!" said Jonathan.

"Um!" said the children, sniffing the air.

The warm air in the bus made the children drowsy. Lights shone in most of the windows of the houses now.

134

Many had one Christmas candle burning in a window. Melissa looked out, and said, "I see a star." Then she yawned.

Miss Adams noticed that Jonathan's head was nodding and his eyes were drooping. She didn't want the children to fall asleep, so she said, "Let's sing a Christmas carol."

Miss Adams began to sing, and Mr. Riley and the children joined in. All but Jonathan. He made believe he was asleep, because he just wanted to smell the Christmas tree and listen. They were singing the same Christmas carol his mother had sung to him the night before, after he had gone to bed. She had sat on the edge of his bed and sung it very softly.

Just as the children finished the last verse, Mr. Riley stopped the bus. "Come, Jonny!" he said. "You're home!"

Jonathan slid off the seat. He stepped over the

135

Christmas tree. He looked back at the tree filling the whole aisle, and said, "It's a big one, isn't it, Rus?"

"It's going to touch the ceiling," Mr. Riley replied. "You just wait and see."

As Jonathan stepped out of the bus, he called back, "Good-by, Rus! Thanks for taking me to cut down the Christmas tree."

"Nice to have you along," said Mr. Riley. "Good night!" The school bus drove off.

The sharp cold awoke Jonathan. As he started up the lane toward his house, he began to hum to himself. It was dark now, but Jonathan could see the lights from the windows of his house, shining softly through the trees.

Jonathan's mother opened the front door to see if her little boy was coming. He had been a long time helping Mr. Riley cut down that Christmas tree. She looked out into the darkness. She didn't see Jonathan, but she heard a small high, sweet voice, singing. She listened and she heard:

Away in a manger
No crib for a bed,
The little Lord Jesus laid down his sweet head.
The stars in the sky looked down where he lay,
The little Lord Jesus asleep in the hay.

Mrs. Mason waited by the front door. When Jonathan saw her, he began to run, kicking through the snow. "Hi, Mommy!" he called out to her. "We cut down the Christmas tree! A great big one! It filled the whole bus!"

Chapter Eight

WALKING ON THE SNOW PILES

ALL DURING the winter one snowstorm followed another. The snow was so deep it covered up the
fences. The snowplows piled the snow along the sides
of the roads until they were like walls. By February the
snow walls were much higher than Jonathan. There

were only two ways he could see over them: when he looked out the windows of the school bus and when he walked on top of them.

All the children liked to walk on top of the snow piles. It was special fun for Jonathan, because he had never had walls of snow to walk on before. It was Jonathan's friend, Melissa Molasses, who first took Jonathan walking on top of the walls of snow. Melissa called it "wall walking," and she was a great wall walker.

Sometimes Melissa came to spend the night at Jonathan's. On these days Jonathan and Melissa got off the school bus together. The next morning they waited for the bus beside the Masons' mailbox. If they got there early, they did a little wall walking.

Jonathan loved to have Melissa come to stay. Melissa had been born on the farm where she lived. She knew many things about the country that Jonathan did not know. She taught Jonathan to know the marks in the snow left by wild animals. Soon he could tell the footprints of the rabbit, the squirrel, the raccoon, the chip-munk, the skunk, and the deer.

Melissa and Jonathan loved to stand on top of the snow piles and look over the white fields, where the snow had become deeper and deeper. Once Melissa pointed to some tracks in the snow left by a fox. Jona-than thought this was very exciting, for he had never lived near a fox before.

Another time, when the children climbed up, Jona-than cried out, "Oh, look, Melissa! Look at those great big tracks in the snow! Some kind of giant animal must have made them." Then he added, "But why didn't he sink in, if he had feet that big? Maybe it's the Abom-inable Snowman!"

Melissa opened her eyes very wide, and said, "What's the Abominable Snowman?"

"Didn't you ever hear of the Abominable Snow-man?" exclaimed Jonathan. Then he said, in a very mysterious way, "Nobody has ever seen him, but they sometimes find his footprints in the snow on some mountain. I think it's in China where they find them, but maybe he has come over here."

Melissa looked down at the footprints. "Silly," she said, "those footprints were left by somebody who walked across the field on snowshoes. You have to wear snowshoes if you want to walk across snow that is as deep as that snow is."

"Oh!" said Jonathan.

"Don't you have snowshoes?" said Melissa.

"No," replied Jonathan. It was not long before Jonathan owned a pair of snowshoes, and he learned to walk in them over the deep snow.

Melissa knew how to do more things with snow than Jonathan had ever dreamed of. They made a snowman out near the mailbox. Jonathan had made snowmen when he had lived in the city, but they had always melted. The snowman that he made with Melissa seemed to get harder and harder. He also grew larger.

After each snowstorm, Jonathan patted new snow all over the snowman. He fixed up the snowman's face and shook the snow off his old hat.

Melissa helped Jonathan build a fort out of snow, and together they dug a cave in the side of a great pile of snow right outside the Masons' house. They made believe that it was an igloo and that they were Eskimos.

Jonathan was beginning to think that the snow would last forever, but as the weeks passed the days grew longer and the sun grew warmer. The great long icicles that hung from the roof of Jonathan's house dripped, drop by drop, during the day and froze again during the night. Patches of paving appeared on the roads where the snow had melted. The firm crust on the walls of snow began to soften under the warmer sun. The children's feet made deeper marks when they walked on top of the piles.

One day, near the end of March, Melissa came home from school with Jonathan. She was going to spend the night. When the school bus stopped at Jonathan's mailbox, both of the children were near the door, ready to jump off. "I'm staying at Jonathan's tonight," Melissa said to Mr. Riley. Then she added, "Rus, you'll be sure to pick up Taffy in the morning, won't you?"

"Sure will!" replied Mr. Riley. "Haven't forgotten him yet, have I?"

"Nope!" said Melissa, as she leaned over and kissed Mr. Riley on his cheek.

As Jonathan and Melissa jumped out of the bus, they called, "Good-by, Rus!"

"Good-by!" Mr. Riley called after them. "See you in the morning. Don't be late."

"Have we ever been late yet?" Melissa called back, laughing.

"Nope!" Mr. Riley replied. He laughed as he closed the door.

The following morning Melissa and Jonathan were

out by the mailbox early. "Let's walk on the wall while we're waiting for the bus," said Jonathan.

"Oh, yes!" said Melissa.

The children scrambled to the top. "It's getting mushy," said Melissa, as her foot broke through the thin crust of ice that had formed during the night.

"Just a little bit," said Jonathan, as he began to run along the top of the pile.

The children walked toward the hill. This way they could watch for the school bus to arrive.

Meanwhile, Mr. Riley was gathering up his busload of children. At some stops one child would be waiting, at others four or five. When he stopped at Melissa's mailbox, Taffy was there. His mother was waiting with him.

Mr. Riley opened the bus door, and called out, "Hi, Taffy! Jump in!"

Taffy's mother gave him a little boost, and Taffy stepped on. "Are we going to get Lissie?" he said.

"Sure are!" replied Mr. Riley. "Pretty soon! Sit down right behind me."

"I don't want to," said Taffy. "I want to sit in the back."

"Why do you want to sit in the back?" said Mr. Riley. "You always sit up front."

"Lissie makes me," said Taffy. "I want to sit in the back."

"All right! Go sit in the back," said Mr. Riley.

Taffy went all the way to the back of the bus. He climbed up on the very last seat and knelt on it, looking out the window.

Mr. Riley drove on, picking up children and getting nearer and nearer to Jonathan's stop.

Suddenly Jonathan and Melissa saw the yellow bus come over the hill. The two children turned around and started to run back to the mailbox. They found it hard to run, because the wet snow stuck to their feet.

"It's getting mushy," Melissa said, once again. No

sooner had she spoken than Melissa began to topple over. She toppled slowly at first. Her left leg went down, down, down, down into the deep snow. Then she fell over into the field beside the road. Now only Melissa's legs in her blue snowpants were sticking out of the snow.

Jonathan leaned over and took hold of one of Melissa's legs. Melissa began to thrash her arms about, trying to reach solid ground. "I'll pull you out, Melissa," Jonathan cried. "I'll pull you out."

As he spoke, Jonathan slid off the snow pile and joined Melissa. Jonathan went backward, but Melissa had toppled over head first.

Jonathan let go of Melissa's leg, so she was able to roll over. Finally her feet touched the earth, and she managed to stand up. She found herself in snow up to her armpits. Jonathan was beside her in the same mess.

As the school bus neared the Masons' stop, Mr. Riley

146

looked for Jonathan and Melissa. He did not see either of the children.

Jonathan and Melissa heard the bus come to a stop. The back end of the bus was just beyond the spot where they were stuck in the snow.

"Well," said Mr. Riley to himself, "they're late!" He honked his horn.

Melissa and Jonathan tried to lift themselves out of the wet snow. The snow was too heavy with water. They were stuck. Melissa opened her mouth, and yelled, "Rus! Rus!"

Rus, inside the bus, could not hear Melissa.

Jonathan yelled, "Help, help!"

Mr. Riley honked his horn again.

"Help, help!" Jonathan and Melissa called out together.

Mr. Riley just honked the horn again.

Taffy, looking out the window, saw Melissa and Jonathan. He thought they were playing in the snow.

He knocked on the window, and called out, "Hi, Lissie! Hi!"

Mr. Riley didn't hear Taffy, because of the noise the horn was making. Melissa did not hear Taffy, and Taffy felt that Melissa wasn't paying any attention to him, so he pounded on the windowpane, and called out again, "Hi, Lissie! Hi!"

Now Mr. Riley heard him. "Keep quiet, Taffy," he said. "Your sister is late, and so is Jonathan."

"There's Lissie!" Taffy called out.

"Where?" said Mr. Riley.

"In the snow," said Taffy.

Mr. Riley went to the door of the bus and looked back. Then he saw the two children. "I'll be there in a second," he called out to them. He got back into his seat. Then he backed the bus until the door was beside the children.

Taffy ran to the front of the bus. Now he was glad to be there. He climbed up on another seat and looked out

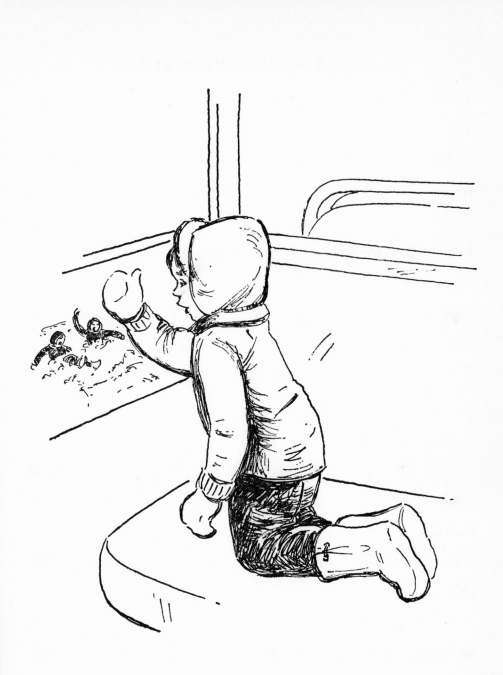

of the window. He looked right down on Melissa and Jonathan. All the children inside the bus were crowded at the windows. "Ooh! Look at Melissa Molasses!" they cried. "Ooh! Look at Jon!" they said.

Mr. Riley leaned over from the step of the bus and held out his arms to Melissa. She took hold of his hands, and he pulled, but Melissa pulled too. Mr. Riley lost his footing, and he fell over the broken pile of snow and joined Melissa and Jonathan.

"Ooh! Ooh!" cried the children in the bus. "Look at Rus!"

All the while Taffy was pounding on the window, calling out, "Hi, Lissie! Hi!"

Mr. Riley stood up in the snow on the other side of the snowbank now. He called up to Taffy, and said, "Stop that. You'll break the window."

Taffy could not hear what Mr. Riley was saying. He went right on pounding, and calling out, "Hi, Lissie! Hi!"

153

Mr. Riley picked up Melissa and shoved her into the bus. Then he picked up Jonathan and pushed him through the door. A great deal of snow came into the bus with the two children, and a great deal more came in with Mr. Riley.

As Mr. Riley sat down at the wheel, Roland Ralston called out, "Wus, Taffy's bleeding." This was followed by screams from Taffy.

Mr. Riley rushed to the screaming boy. "Did you break the window?" he asked.

"No, he didn't break the window," said Roland. "He cut his hand on a piece of tin he has in his pocket."

Taffy held up his hand and screamed louder. The bus driver put his hand into his pocket and pulled out a Band-aid. He put it around Taffy's finger, and said, "You should be glad you didn't cut your hand off. Didn't I tell you to stop pounding on that window?"

"But Lissie wouldn't look at me," said Taffy.

Melissa sat down beside her little brother. She put

her arm around him. "Why wouldn't you look at me, Lissie?" said Taffy.

"I was busy," said Melissa.

Mr. Riley started the bus on its way again. "What a morning!" he said.

Chapter Nine

THE PET SHOW

SPRING HAD come at last. Even before the last patches of snow had disappeared, the tiny buds on the willow trees were golden. Soon the maples had turned their dark gray branches to a soft pink. More birds appeared at the feeder beside the Masons' back porch.

A thick gooey mud followed the spring thaw. It almost pulled Jonathan's rubbers off as he went to meet the school bus. Then the mud dried up, and Jonathan could run to the mailbox again.

The children took off their mittens, their scarves, their hoods, and their caps. They took them off wherever they happened to be. Mr. Riley gathered up the things the children left on the bus every day. Sometimes the mittens and scarves and hoods and caps rode around in the bus for days and days. The children seemed to forget that they had ever worn them.

One day after school, when Mr. Riley picked up the children, they had news for him. "We're going to have a Pet Show at school," said Jonathan, who was at the head of the line.

"Yes!" Melissa called out. "Isn't that nice, Rus? We're going to bring all our pets."

"And there will be prizes," said another girl, named Janet. "I bet my Sweet Pea will get one."

157

"It isn't a Flower Show, silly!" said Melissa.

"Well, my Sweet Pea isn't a flower," said Janet.

Mr. Riley looked down at the children, and said, "Do you mean that I have to pick up your pets along with the rest of you?"

"We can't walk our pets to school," said Melissa. "It's too far."

"Well, that will be a day!" said Mr. Riley. "I'll have to eat my spinach to get ready for that day."

The children laughed. "It will be fun!" said Jonathan. "I'm going to bring Cocoa."

"I'm going to bring my goldfish," said Melissa.

This started the whole line of children talking about their pets. Nearly every child who stepped into the bus told Mr. Riley about the pet he intended to bring to school for the Pet Show.

"I'll be carrying a traveling zoo!" exclaimed Mr. Riley. "When is this going to be?"

"The day school closes for the Easter vacation," said Miss Adams, who was standing beside the bus.

The day before the Pet Show Mr. Riley went into the school to talk to the children. "Now," he said, "I want you all to listen very carefully. Tomorrow morning many of you children will be getting on the bus with a pet. I want you to remember that all dogs must be on a leash. If you get on with a dog, you must take it to the back of the bus. All cats must have a collar and a leash. If you get on with a cat, you must sit up front."

"Where do turtles go?" said Rocky.

"I'm coming to them," said Mr. Riley. "All turtles and goldfish must sit in the middle of the bus."

"What about rabbits?" said Buddy Miller.

"And hamsters?" said another boy.

"And ducks?" said a girl named Daisy.

"Ducks!" exclaimed Mr. Riley. "I hadn't thought of ducks!"

Several voices called out, "Oh, I have a duck!"

"Well then!" said Mr. Riley. "Ducks, rabbits, and hamsters go with the turtles and goldfish. Be careful not to break the bowls and don't have too much water in them."

"Do the ducks have to come in bowls with water?" asked Daisy.

"Ducks, rabbits, and hamsters have to come in boxes," said Mr. Riley.

"Oh!" said Daisy.

"Now I hope this is all clear," said Mr. Riley. "Just remember! Dogs in the back, cats in the front, and everything else in the middle. Turtles and fish in bowls. Everything else in boxes."

"Don't I bring my parakeet in its cage?" said Margie.

"Oh yes, yes!" said Mr. Riley. "I forgot about birds. Birds in cages."

The following morning Jonathan and Cocoa stood by the mailbox, waiting for the bus. Cocoa was on his leash. When the bus arrived, it sounded like a dog-catcher's wagon. All the big dogs were barking. All the little dogs were yapping.

Mr. Riley opened the door and called out, "Come along, Jonny. Just what this bus needs is one more dog. Come along!"

Instead of jumping into the bus, Cocoa hung back. "Come on, Cocoa!" said Jonathan, giving a tug on the leash.

Cocoa lay down flat on his stomach. For months he had tried to get on the bus with Jonathan. Now that he was invited, he didn't want to go. Jonathan pulled. "Come on, Cocoa!" he said.

Cocoa just rolled his eyes. "Cocoa, come on!" said Jonathan.

"Pick him up," said Mr. Riley. "Pick him up."

Jonathan picked up Cocoa and stepped into the bus.

"Carry him to the back," said Mr. Riley.

Jonathan could feel Cocoa trembling. "He's scared!" said Jonathan to Mr. Riley.

"Well, so am I!" replied Mr. Riley. "I never drove a Noah's ark before."

"Hi, Jon!" Melissa called out from the center of the bus. She was holding her goldfish bowl on her lap. A single goldfish was swimming in the water in the bowl. "See my goldfish?" she said.

Jonathan stopped to look at Melissa's goldfish. As he did so, Cocoa jumped out of his arms. He jumped right down on the goldfish bowl and knocked it off Melissa's lap. The bowl crashed at her feet. The water splashed all over her. It splashed into the box of ducks that Daisy was holding on her lap.

Daisy cried, "Oh, my ducks!"

Melissa cried, "Oh, my fish!"

Jonathan cried, "Oh, Cocoa!"

162

The ducks shook themselves. The goldfish landed on the floor. Cocoa started to fight with a pug dog.

Mr. Riley heard the crash of the fish bowl. He stopped the bus and came back to see what the trouble was. "Oh, Rus!" cried Melissa. "Look at my poor goldfish."

"Just a minute, Melissa!" said Mr. Riley. "I'll put your fish into Walter's fish bowl." Walter was sitting across the aisle holding a fish bowl with five fish.

"No, no!" cried Melissa. "I won't be able to tell which is my fish and which are Walter's."

The little fish was flapping around on the floor, and Mr. Riley knew that something would have to be done quickly. He put his hand in his pocket and pulled out a sandwich. The sandwich was inside a plastic bag. He took the sandwich out of the plastic bag and put it back in his pocket. Then he said to Melissa, "You hold the bag and I'll pour what is left of this water into it."

Melissa held the bag, and Mr. Riley poured the little

water that was left in the broken bowl into the bag. Then he picked up the goldfish and dropped it into the bag. "Now hold on to it," he said to Melissa.

"Is he still alive?" said Melissa.

"Yes, he's still alive," replied Mr. Riley, picking up the pieces of glass. He carried the pieces of glass to the front of the bus and put them in a trash bag. Then he started the bus again.

In a few minutes, Melissa cried out, "Rus! I think my goldfish is dead."

"Is it floating on top of the water?" Mr. Riley called back.

"No!" said Melissa.

"Then it isn't dead," said Mr. Riley.

In another minute, Melissa called out, "Rus! I think this bag has a hole in it."

"The bag is all right," replied Mr. Riley, as he swung the bus around a corner to pick up Janet.

To Mr. Riley's great surprise, there stood Janet with

a big sheep. She had a blue satin ribbon tied around its neck. Janet was holding on to the two ends of the ribbon. Mr. Riley opened the door, and called out, "No sheep, Janet! No sheep!"

"But this is Sweet Pea!" said Janet. "She's the only pet I have."

"But I can't take that big thing in this bus," said Mr. Riley.

Janet began to cry. "But she's the only pet I have," she sobbed.

"All right! All right!" said Mr. Riley. "Put her on."

Sweet Pea jumped in as though she was quite used to going to school on the bus. "Stay right up in front with her," said Mr. Riley.

"She'll be good," said Janet. "She doesn't mind cats."

"If I see anybody waiting for the bus with a cow," said Mr. Riley, "I'm going to drive right by."

"Rus!" Melissa called out. "Water is dripping out of the bag."

"Well, pinch it!" Mr. Riley called back.

Mr. Riley picked up more and more children. They all had to push past Sweet Pea. The ones with pets found this harder than the ones who didn't have pets. The dogs barked at Sweet Pea and the cats spit.

Just as Mr. Riley swung the bus into the school grounds, Rocky called out, "Rus, I've lost Casey!"

"Who is Casey?" Mr. Riley called back.

"My turtle!" said Rocky.

"I didn't see you get on with a turtle," said Mr. Riley.

"He was in my pocket," replied Rocky.

"When everybody gets out of the bus, I'll help you look for your turtle," said Mr. Riley.

As Melissa was about to step out of the bus, she said, "Rus, what shall I do with my goldfish now?"

"Oh, Miss Adams will give you a jar to put it in," replied Mr. Riley.

"I'll save the bag for you, Rus," said Melissa. "So you can put your sandwich back in it."

"No, thanks!" replied Mr. Riley, as he pulled Rocky's turtle out from under a pile of lost mittens, scarves, caps, and hoods.

When the pet show was over, Mr. Riley had to take the children and their pets back to their homes. Jonathan was at the head of the line with Cocoa, waiting to get on the bus. When he saw Mr. Riley, he said, "What do you think, Rus! Cocoa won the prize for the best dog."

"Good for Cocoa!" said Mr. Riley.

"Miss Adams gave me a jar for my goldfish," said Melissa. "But he didn't get a prize. A black one got the prize, and I don't think it's fair. A black fish isn't a goldfish, is it, Rus?"

"It is if the judges say so," replied Mr. Riley.

"Rus!" said Janet, as she stepped into the bus with her sheep. "Guess what! Sweet Pea won the prize for the best of all the animals in the Pet Show. She got the blue ribbon!"

"That's fine!" said Mr. Riley. "Now if I get you all home with this menagerie, I hope someone will give me a prize!"

Chapter Ten

A SURPRISE FOR JONATHAN

IT WAS June. Now the school bus drove past green fields. Daisies and buttercups grew beside the roads. The sun shining through the leaves of the tall elm trees made shadow patterns on the road. Soon school would close for the long summer vacation. Jonathan's first year in his new school would be over.

171

One morning Jonathan was riding on the hot seat, beside Mr. Riley. "This seat isn't very hot any more," said Jonathan.

"Not at this time of the year," replied Mr. Riley.

"I was afraid to sit on it the first time," said Jonathan. "Remember?"

"Yes, I remember," said Mr. Riley.

"It was nice in the wintertime," said Jonathan.

"Will you be glad when school is over?" Mr. Riley asked.

"I guess so," said Jonathan. "I guess there will be lots of things to do."

"You don't sound too sure," said Mr. Riley.

"Well, I won't be riding on the bus," said Jonathan, "and I like to ride on this bus."

"I'm glad you do, Jonny," said Mr. Riley. "I like having you."

"What will you do, Rus, when we don't have school?" Jonathan asked.

"Oh, I drive a taxicab in the summer," Mr. Riley replied.

While Jonathan chattered, Mr. Riley stopped to pick up the children. When the bus stopped for Janet, Sweet Pea was waiting with Janet.

"There's Sweet Pea!" the children in the bus called out.

"I guess she likes to ride on the bus, too," said Jonathan.

Sweet Pea had waited for the bus every morning since the Pet Show. Every morning she had to be chased home. Sometimes Mr. Riley had to get out of the bus and chase her. This morning Janet's mother called Sweet Pea, so Mr. Riley did not have to leave his wheel.

When Janet got into the bus, she handed Mr. Riley a little bunch of flowers. "I picked these for you, Rus," she said.

"Isn't that nice!" said Mr. Riley, taking the bunch of

flowers from Janet. "I'll put them in water when I get home." He drove on.

"Well, as I was saying," said Jonathan to Mr. Riley, "I like to ride. I like to go all around the country. I like to see everything."

"I see!" said Mr. Riley.

The next stop was Walter's. At Walter's there was a brown horse. The horse's name was Brownie. Brownie was in the pasture every morning now. He knew the school bus just as Sweet Pea did, even though Brownie had never been on it.

Nearly every morning Brownie walked over to the bus, when it stopped to pick up Walter. All the children looked for the horse. They called out, "There's Brownie!" "Here comes Brownie!" "Here comes Brownie!" "Hello, Brownie!"

This morning Brownie was very near the door when Mr. Riley opened it. "Can I pat him, Rus?" said Melissa, who was sitting in the front seat.

"Of course not!" said Mr. Riley. "We have to get to school. We can't stop while you pat horses."

Walter stepped into the bus. He was carrying a big red apple. "Good morning, Walter!" said Mr. Riley. "You look all slicked up this morning."

"My mother cut my hair," said Walter. Then he held out the apple, and said, "I was going to give this apple to Brownie, but it was such a pretty one I saved it for you, Rus." He rubbed the apple on his trousers. "I'll shine it up for you."

"Thank you, Walter!" said Mr. Riley. "That's wonderful of you." Walter handed the apple to Mr. Riley, who took a large bite out of it right away. "Good apple!" he said.

"Well, as I was saying," said Jonathan.

"That's right, Jonny!" said Mr. Riley. "Tell me some more."

"Did you know that I'm going to be a bus driver when I grow up?" said Jonathan.

"You don't say!" exclaimed Mr. Riley, between two bites of his apple. "A school bus driver?"

"That's right," said Jonathan.

"That won't be very soon," said Mr. Riley.

"Well, I'm going to," said Jonathan, " 'cause I like to go around and see everything. I like to see animals like Sweet Pea and Brownie, and I like to see people, too."

Soon the bus stopped for Buddy Miller. "Hi, Buddy!" said Mr. Riley, as the door opened. Buddy was carrying a box and his eyes were shining. "What have you got there?" said Mr. Riley.

"It's for you," said Buddy. "My mother made you some fudge."

"Fudge!" exclaimed Mr. Riley. "Do I love fudge!" He took the box from Buddy, and said, "Thank you, Buddy! Thank you very much." He put the box of fudge on the floor beside his seat.

As Mr. Riley started the bus again, Jonathan said,

"Rus, shall I tell you another reason why I think it is nice to be a bus driver?"

"Go right ahead," said Mr. Riley. "I'd like to hear it."

"Well, people are always giving you things," said Jonathan.

"That's right!" said Mr. Riley. "It's Christmas all the time."

"But you wouldn't get presents if you weren't a nice bus driver," said Jonathan. "You have to be a nice bus driver, like you, Rus."

"Thanks, Jonny, thanks!" said Mr. Riley. "It isn't hard to be nice to you boys and girls. Even when I have to take all your animals along and pull you out of snowdrifts and find your turtles and your mittens and scarves and caps."

"And find my birthday cake," said Jonathan.

Mr. Riley laughed and finished his apple.

" 'Course it would be nice to drive an ice-cream

truck," said Jonathan, "and stop at all the places that sell ice cream. Carry it in and put it in those big chests they always have for ice cream."

"Well, maybe you could drive a school bus in the winter, and an ice-cream truck in the summer," said Mr. Riley.

"That's a good idea!" said Jonathan. "I think I'd like that. Why don't you do that, Rus? Then maybe you would get to taste the ice cream."

"My brother is driving an ice-cream truck now," said Mr. Riley, as he swung the bus up near the door of the school. "He used to be a milkman."

Melissa was the first to get off the bus. She stopped beside Mr. Riley and said, "I didn't have any present for you this morning, but I can give you a kiss."

"Lovely, lovely! Melissa Molasses, the Kissing Bug!" said Mr. Riley. "Put it right here on my cheek." Melissa put a kiss on Mr. Riley's cheek and jumped out of the bus.

"You know something, Rus?" said Jonathan, as he left the hot seat. "Where I lived before, I used to go out with the milkman in his truck. And do you know what his name—"

"Look, Jonny! Get out! You're the last one," said Mr. Riley.

"But I want to tell you this," said Jonathan.

"Tell it to me on the way home," said Mr. Riley.

In the middle of the morning Miss Adams asked Jonathan to take a message to the office. The office was around the corner at the end of the hall. She wrote a note and gave it to him.

Jonathan went out of the room and turned down the hall. At the very end of the hall, there was a door leading out of the building. As Jonathan neared the door, he could see the ice-cream truck standing outside. He knew then that the ice cream was being delivered to the lunchroom.

Suddenly the door opened and a man came into the

building carrying some large cans of ice cream. The light was behind the man so that Jonathan could not see his face. He was all dark in the strong light of the open door. When the man saw Jonathan, he stopped and called out, "Why, Jonny! What are you doing here?"

Jonathan walked up to the man. Now he could see his face, and he said, "Hello, Mr. Riley! I'm taking a note to the office for Miss Adams."

"But when did you come here?" the man asked.

"Why, you know, I came on the bus this morning," replied Jonathan. "You brought me."

"Oh, Jonny!" said the man. "That's my twin brother who drives the school bus. Don't you remember me? You used to go riding in the milk truck with me."

"Oh, Mr. Riley!" said Jonathan. "Are you the ice-cream man now?"

"That's right!" replied Mr. Riley. "I gave up that

184

job where you used to live. I decided to come up here and be near my brother."

"Oh, Mr. Riley! I'm glad to see you," said Jonathan.

"Maybe you would like to go riding with me again after school closes," said Mr. Riley.

"Oh, Mr. Riley!" said Jonathan. "That would be wonderful!"

"Just call me Bud," said Mr. Riley.

Jonathan was so excited he forgot to take the note to the office. Instead he carried it back to Miss Adams. "Why, Jon!" she said. "I told you to take the note to the office."

"Oh, yes!" said Jonathan.

Jonathan turned and ran down the hall to the office. He handed the note to a lady sitting behind a desk and turned away quickly. Out in the hall he met Mr. Riley again. He was leaving with some empty ice-cream cans. "See you soon!" said Mr. Riley.

"I'll be waiting for you, Bud!" said Jonathan. "Do you know where I live?"

"I'll find out from Rus," Mr. Riley called. "Don't worry! I'll find you. Good-by, Jonny!"

"Good-by, Bud!" Jonathan called back.

CAROLYN HAYWOOD is distinguished both as author and illustrator of children's books. Her first book was published in 1939. Since then she has had many other books published and has become one of the most widely read American writers for younger children.

Carolyn Haywood was born in Philadelphia and still lives in that city. She is a graduate of the Philadelphia Normal School and studied at the Pennsylvania Academy of Fine Arts, where she won the Cresson European Scholarship for distinguished work. Miss Haywood calls herself a "grand-pupil" of the great American illustrator, Howard Pyle, having studied with three of his distinguished pupils, Elizabeth Shippen Green Elliott, Violet Oakley, and Jessie Willcox Smith. She is also a portrait painter and has specialized in portraits of children. Her experience in this field has given her a sympathetic understanding of children and their interests which has made her peculiarly well fitted to write and illustrate for them. She is continuing her portrait work with commissions in New York, Philadelphia, and other eastern cities.

Miss Haywood has published twenty-four books, all of which she has illustrated herself.